CIARA GER

THE
THAT

Ciara Geraghty is the author of five books: *Saving Grace, Becoming Scarlett, Finding Mr Flood, Lifesaving for Beginners,* and *Now That I've Found You.* She has one husband, three children and a dog.

You can find out more at www.ciarageraghty.com, visit her Facebook page at www.facebook.com/pages/CiaraGeraghtyBooks, or follow her on Twitter @ciarageraghty.

NEW ISLAND

THE STORIES THAT REMAIN
First published 2015
by New Island
16 Priory Office Park
Stillorgan
Co Dublin

www.newisland.ie

PRINT ISBN: 978-1-84840-413-7

British Library Cataloguing Data. A CIP catalogue record
for this book is available from the British Library

Typeset by JVR Creative India
Cover design by New Island Books
Printed by SPRINT-print Ltd.

New Island received financial assistance from
The Arts Council (*An Comhairle Ealaíon*), Dublin, Ireland

10 9 8 7 6 5 4 3 2 1

Dear Reader,

On behalf of myself and the other contributing authors, I would like to welcome you to the eighth Open Door series. The books in this series are written and designed to introduce new and emergent readers to the writings of many bestselling authors who have sold millions of books worldwide. We hope that you enjoy the books and that reading becomes a lasting pleasure in your life.

Warmest wishes,

Patricia Scanlan.

Patricia Scanlan
Series Editor

Please visit www.newisland.ie for information on all eight Open Door series.

This story is inspired by Peggy Mangen and her faithful dog, Casper, and dedicated to their memories.

It is also dedicated to my father, Don Geraghty, who never forgets to love us.

Chapter One

There are things he remembers.

My lead, for example. The scented bags for, let us say, accidents. His cigarettes. He puts the lighter in the back pocket of his trousers but he pats the breast pocket of his shirt first. When he's looking for it.

Every time.

I don't think he remembers my name. George. That is me. It is forgettable enough, George. I suppose I should be grateful that I didn't end up as a 'Fluffy' or 'Scamp'. Or, God forbid,

'Barbie' like that poor mutt in number fifty-seven. May the Good Lord save me from a moniker like that!

A bit of dignity in a George, all the same.

He kneels beside me when he clips the lead onto my collar. I hear the creak and crackle of his bones. Well, we are not getting any younger. He puts his hands over my ears and rubs them. Then he grips the rail of the banisters and uses it to pull himself up.

The wind whips through the hall when he opens the front door. His jacket is draped across the hall table. Mrs Bolton leaves it there for him. He puts it on and zips it up. He looks cold already. His fingers are stiff and white. She is right. Those cigarettes will be the death of him, with his sluggish circulation.

'Come on, boy,' he says, making that clicking sound the people make with their tongue. I don't know why they do that. I haven't met a fellow canine yet who owns to liking it. I wag my tail anyway. They like it when we do that. He smiles. Not the big, wide smile he had. It is a small smile now, the memory of a smile. He bends, pulls at one of my ears, pats my head. His breath smells of coffee, gone cold.

'Where are you off to now?' Mrs Bolton pokes her head around the kitchen door. She has opened it a crack, so as not to let the heat out.

'The shops,' he says.

'Have you got your keys?'

'Yes.' He doesn't. There they are, hanging on the hook that he hammered into the wall years ago.

Mrs Bolton nods. She knows he doesn't have his keys but she asks anyway. Habit, I suppose. Or perhaps she hopes for some small change in this conversation. No matter. She'll be here to let us in. She always is.

'Don't forget your hat. It is perishing out there.' She nods towards the pocket of his jacket. He looks down, slides his hand into the slit and finds the hat. He holds it up, like it is a trophy he used to win in those golf tournaments at the club. A six handicap, he had. He was good. He'd drop that into conversations whenever he got a chance. That, and the hole-in-one story. I could recite that particular tale word for word.

Mrs Bolton glances at me, then back at Mr B. 'Take care,' she says.

It is a dull day. Dry, but the rain is a matter of when rather than if, judging by that stiff wind and the dark underbelly of cloud edging in from the west. My nails scrape against the pavement. I haven't been to *The Pampered Pooch* for a while. They claim to specialise in King Charles Spaniels, although although I've seen other breeds. Matilda gives us all the same treatment. She's capable, Matilda, which is a quality I admire. She does a great job on my nails, but she has a heavy hand with that foul-smelling anti-flea spray. *As if!*

Our usual route is a loop, from the house to the shop. He buys Silk Cut Blue and the occasional bag of Allsorts. Then it is time to go back home. We turn left at the top of the street, round the corner, cross the road and out onto Texas Lane. That overweight Labrador – an unimaginative 'Leo' – at number twenty-two waddles down his driveway. He cocks his leg at the pillar, then hauls himself along to the pillar outside number twenty-four. He sniffs it and raises his leg again. I really think one should pick a specific place for attending to one's business. My spot is behind the shed in the back garden, which affords both privacy *and* dignity.

We stop at the pillar recently sullied by Leo. Mr B reaches into various pockets until he locates his handkerchief. He mops the perspiration from his brow, despite the chill in the air.

'Looks like rain,' says Mrs Byrne, who is walking towards us. The wheels of her shopping bag squeak like mice. 'WD-40,' Mr B would have said, back in the day. He would have oiled the wheels himself. Insisted on it. Now, he nods and puts the handkerchief back in his pocket. 'Terrible business,' she goes on. 'That factory in Swords closing. More jobs lost. I don't know what this country is coming to.'

He shakes his head. 'Terrible business,' he says. It is clever really, how he does it. Repeats what the person has said. A phrase. A couple of words. Nods. Or shakes his head. Smiles sometimes. Or looks grave, like Mrs Byrne. He mirrors them. A reflection.

Mrs Byrne nods, satisfied. 'They won't be happy until all our young people are gone. Or on the dole.'

'Indeed they won't.' He nods, looks grave.

This is how he manages. This is how he makes it through his days.

Chapter Two

The funny thing is, the Boltons never wanted a dog. Especially Mr B. The children begged them, the way children do. I've heard the stories around the dinner table. He was adamant. No pets. He didn't have time back then. A lot of overtime in those days, at the airport.

Mr B liked telling stories. One might say he fancied himself as a bit of a comedian. He was always called upon to tell a joke at family gatherings. He told stories, rather than jokes. But they were amusing all the same. That was the first hint of it. Oh, years ago now. Clara's thirtieth birthday. Mrs Bolton made chocolate cake. Peter came with his first wife and their two little girls, who petted me excessively. They tied their hair ribbons around my neck and pulled me through the house. They claimed they were 'training' me.

After a while came the usual line from Mr B. 'Did I ever tell you the story about the Cavan man going to Dublin and staying at the Greshham hotel?' Groans from everyone, even the little girls, schooled well by their father.

'You've only told us about a hundred times,' said Mrs Bolton briskly, but smiling at him. Softened by the warmth of the room filled with her children and grandchildren, and the second glass of wine.

He got close to the end of the story and then he stopped and frowned and shook his head, like he was disagreeing with somebody. He picked up his glass and drank deeply from it. He drank rather a lot back then. 'Go on, Ted,' said Mrs Bolton. Her expression was impatient but there was something else there. An inkling perhaps, gaining momentum. Maybe she already knew.

'Excuse me a moment,' he said, replacing his glass on the table and moving towards the dining room door. 'I just need to . . .' and then he was gone. By the time he came back, everybody had forgotten about the Cavan man and the Gresham hotel. They didn't ask what it was that Mr B had just needed to do. Mrs Bolton served dessert – her signature peach pavlova – and Mr B made coffee because nobody else knew how to use the complicated machine he had bought after he retired.

But pardon me, I'm rambling. The thing was, the Boltons didn't want a dog.

And then my mother died giving birth to me and my siblings. Our owner – Miss Cavendish – put all six of us into a sack. She secured the top with the rope of an ancient, fading dressing gown hanging from a hook on the back of the bathroom door. She dragged the sack with her skeletal, age-spotted hands, to the bottom of her garden. Then she pushed it into the Broadmeadow River at Rolestown. There was a tiny hole in the bottom of the sack which saved us. Well, me at least. I can't be certain what happened to the others. It is a cause for regret, of course. But at the time, I was concerned only with survival. I ended up in Malahide. I huddled on moss-covered stones at the water's edge, surrounded by vast seagulls. I could see myself in their glassy black eyes as they circled closer. The way Mr B tells it, I was at death's door, although he can be prone to overdoing it for the sake of a story.

Why, you might very well wonder? Why did Miss Cavendish dispose of my three brothers, two sisters and I in that manner? Why did Mr B pick me up and wrap me in his scarf that day? And why did Mrs Bolton not insist that he take me back to where he'd found me, instead of making a makeshift bed for me in the corner of the kitchen, beside the Aga. A shoebox, with a towel tucked inside. 'It is only temporary, mind,' she said, nodding towards me. 'We can send him to Dogs Trust when he's a little stronger. They'll find a good home for him, I'm sure.' Her voice was sharp and high. Mr B took her hand and when she smiled, it was so unexpected. Like a lamb bone on a Tuesday. It transformed her face. Revealed her grace. Her beauty.

When I got too big for the box, she bought me a basket. A fine, wicker one.

Why? One could spend a great deal of time trying to answer that question. I think perhaps that sometimes there *is* no why. No reason why things happen. What I *do* know is that Mrs Bolton never mentioned Dogs Trust again.

Chapter Three

Mr B has forgotten his wallet. Mrs O'Connell at the newsagents hands him the packet of cigarettes anyway. 'Do you have your lighter?' She asks and he pats the breast pocket of his shirt before pushing his hand into the back pocket of his trousers and nodding.

'The Merry Widow', Mr B used to call her. Because of her sunny nature, I assume. That, and the fact that her husband left her a huge amount of stocks and shares when the bone cancer got the upper hand. People wonder why she continues to stand behind the counter. I'd say it is the comfort of knowing everyone's business. 'I'll get Mrs Bolton to settle the account when she's in again,' Mrs O'Connell says, making a note of the transaction on the back of a brown envelope.

Mr B slips the cigarettes into his jacket pocket. 'Indeed,' he says, and smiles a goodbye. Outside, he stands still for a moment, looks left and right as if he's getting ready to cross a road. 'Come on, boy.' He pulls at the lead and turns towards right instead of left. Now we are walking through an estate that leads to the Dublin Road, instead of back the way we came, along Yellow Walls Road, as is our routine.

Perhaps he wants to stretch his legs a little more? Although it is hardly the weather for it. I follow behind him.

If you met him in a library, for example, or in a public house perhaps.

If you spoke to him for five minutes. If you stood beside him in a queue at the bank machine, say. You wouldn't know.

You would see a man. You might think he was in his mid-sixties, even though he will be seventy-two next spring. It is his hair, I imagine. Still there. And while the colour has changed over the years, the grey that has replaced the black is steel rather than pale. It lends him a resolve that people relate to youth. He is tall and thin. Getting thinner, too. Mrs Bolton serves his usual portions but when she is distracted by an item on the six o'clock news, he pushes the mound of potato into a tissue. He wraps the tissue around the food. He hides it in his pocket. Sometimes, he remembers to flush the tissue down the toilet. Or put it in the bin. Often the wrong-coloured bin. Sometimes he doesn't remember. Mrs Bolton finds them when she does the laundry. The neighbours have front-row seats on those days! I'm sure they wonder why she continues to berate him. Why she asks him the same things over and over, as if it is she who is losing her memory.

What were you thinking?

You can't do that!

We'll be infested with mice at this rate!

Maybe she is afraid. Of the day when she finds the potatoes, or the peas, or the pieces of meat, wrapped in tissue paper in his trousers pocket. The day when she doesn't shout. Doesn't berate him. The day when she lifts the soggy tissue out of the pocket and puts it in the bin. Puts the trousers in the washing machine. Turns the machine on and goes about her daily business as if nothing odd has happened. As if this is normal. No need to pause. To rant and rail.

Perhaps that is the day she dreads.

A thin drizzle has begun. To the west, a bank of cloud lowers, blackens, gathers momentum. Mr B pulls at the collar of his jacket, blows into one hand, then the other. We clear the estate and reach the Dublin Road and he pauses for a moment. I strain to the left, towards home, the lead taut between us. We are not an intimidating breed, I'll grant you, but there is strength in our bodies all the same. Mr B has to yank the lead with both hands before I give in.

We turn right, down the Dublin Road, with Malahide, and home, behind us now.

Chapter Four

His phone rings for the first time as we turn onto the Swords Road. He strides along as if he is once again a man with someplace to be. As if he cannot hear his phone. As if it is not ringing at all. His breath is loud and erupts from his mouth in white clouds. So is mine. It is true to say we are walking faster – and farther – than we have done in years. In my mind's eye, I see Mrs Bolton with her phone to her ear, twitching the net curtains in the front room, peering up the road, examining her watch. She's talking to herself. Sometimes she does that when she's alone in the house, when Peter brings Mr B out for a drive. She's shaking her head and saying, 'He should be back by now.' Looking at her watch and shaking her head. She will say it again, as if whoever she is talking to might not have heard her the first time. 'He should be back by now.'

Forty-five years they've been married. Sapphire. That is the traditional gift for forty-five years of wedlock. I know because one of the women Mrs Bolton plays bridge with told her, when she called at the door to deliver the hamper Mrs Bolton had won at the last competition. 'Sapphire,' she told her, in her booming, matter-of-fact voice. 'A beautiful stone. Make sure you tell him. You know what the men are like, hopeless at that kind of thing.' Mrs Bolton smiled, but of course she didn't tell Mr B about the sapphires. Nor did she mention the anniversary. He has the date written on a piece of paper the garage where he goes to smoke, '30th of September'. The problem is he forgets to look at the piece of paper. He always answers 'Bertie,' when the consultant asks him who is the leader of the government. Mr Ahern hasn't been in government since 2008, thank goodness.

Mrs Bolton coaches him before he goes for his check-ups. 'It is Tuesday, the twenty-seventh of June,' she whispers in the waiting room. 'The president of America is Barack Obama. It is 2014, JUNE. Okay?' He smiles at her when she tells him these facts. An indulgent smile, like he's humouring her. I'm not fond of going to the appointments but Mr B has got it into his head that it is not safe to leave me alone in the house anymore. Mrs Bolton is none too pleased but Mr Murphy, the consultant, pats my head. He says he's a dog person.

Mrs Bolton needed both hands to carry the hamper into the kitchen. She is an excellent bridge player, although she wouldn't agree. Some people never know the measure of themselves, I suppose.

The clocks went back last week. That, coupled with the shadow thrown by the clouds, almost overhead now, drains the light of the day and turns the dregs of afternoon into evening. At the roundabout outside the Pavillions on the N1, Mr B turns left and continues walking. We're on the hard shoulder of the dual carriageway. The rush-hour traffic roars past us, lifting puddles of rainwater into arcs of fine spray. It looks almost beautiful through the filter of the orange street lights. The water settles on my fur.

We're headed towards Dublin airport. The drone of airplane engines is loud, even over the noise of the traffic. When he hears one, Mr B lifts his head and says, 'Airbus 330, I'd say,' or, 'That must be a little Cessna.' He can't see them through the clouds. He works it out by their sound. I don't know if he's accurate but if I were a betting soul, I'd put a vet's bank account on him. He worked at Dublin airport for thirty-three years. In the hangars which, I gather, is the place where the airplanes are stored while they are being serviced and repaired. 'Birds,' Mr B calls them. 'She's a big bird,' he'll say when the jumbo passes overhead.

Mr B used to have an endless supply of stories about his time at Dublin Airport. Now it is just a handful. Three, maybe. The others have leaked away, like rainwater down a drain. He tells the stories that remain often, to whoever will listen. I imagine it is his way of keeping them. Making sure he doesn't lose these last few. Peter heads him off at the pass, 'I heard that one before.' Clara listens like it is the first time. She laughs in the pauses he creates for such purpose, as the stories are funny. Or at least they used to be, when he first told them. In these remaining stories, he remembers the month and the year. He remembers the names of his workmates. The nicknames. Flippin' Jemmy (rampant curser). Two-time Terry (serial adulterer). Dial M for Malcolm (always on the phone). He remembers where the stories took place. In hangar one or hangar two or his office, a cluttered little room off at the side.

The rain arrives, lashing against us in slanted lines, helped by the wind which has grown stronger and sharper. I've never had a nervous disposition but I have to admit to an increasing sense of worry. The bright lights of Dublin Airport glow to our right but Mr B continues straight on down the road, towards Santry. Santry is where Mrs Bolton first worked after she got her book-keeping certificate. 'There,' she sometimes says when we drive past a piece of waste ground where the office used to be. 'Hard to believe it was so long ago.' When it is just me in the car, she might take one hand off the steering wheel and place it on my head, shaking her head at the years and how they have gone by.

When Mr B stops to examine our surroundings, I bend my head and lap at a puddle of rainwater which, I assure you, is not an activity in which I usually indulge. We both notice the public house at the same time. Kealy's. It was here that Mr B went the morning he signed his early retirement contract and got 'the lump' as he called it. The suits who brokered the deal told him there was no hurry. He could go home. Think about it. Discuss it with his family. He picked up the pen and asked them where he should sign. Then he went straight to Kealy's for a pint. Or a number of pints, if I know Mr B, and let's face it, I do.

That is one of the stories that remain. The early retirement one. The 'Where do I sign?' one. Possibly his favourite, if the regularity with which he tells it is an indication.

We cross the road and I am relieved to see that the traffic has thinned out because there are no pedestrian crossings. Mr B's clothes are dark and I'm too low to the ground to be of any assistance, when it comes to visibility. King Charles Spaniels may be an elegant breed but we are none too lofty. More's the pity.

There is a man outside the door of the pub, where a makeshift canopy shelters him from the worst of the rain as he smokes. Mr B stands beside him and takes out his cigarettes. He begins to pat at his various pockets when the man extends his hand and rolls his thumb along the wheel of a cheap Bic lighter. He offers the flame to Mr B, who bends his head towards it. I am grateful that memory has no place among these rituals. Mr B straightens and exhales the smoke in a long thin line. He smiles his thanks, which the man accepts with a nod.

'Good night for ducks,' the man says, lighting another cigarette.

'Ducks?' Mr B looks confused.

The man twitches his head at the rain. 'The rain,' he says.

'Oh. Yes. The rain,' says Mr B.

'Still, the mutts have to be walked, regardless of the elements, right?' He points at me with a fat, nicotine-stained finger. *Mutt indeed.*

'Do you work at the airport?' Mr B asks, brushing raindrops off his jacket.

'The airport? No, I'm a . . .'

'Thirty-three years I was there. Some of the best days I had, at the airport. And in Kealy's, of course.'

The man smiles as if he too had some of his best days in Kealy's. Perhaps he did.

'Tony won't let you bring the mutt inside, you know. He's not as easy going since he gave up the gargle.'

'Inside?'

The man tosses his head towards the door. 'You going in for a pint, yeah?'

'Oh. No, no I'm . . . we're just passing. Haven't been inside the place in years. Not since . . .' He frowns, shakes his head. He looks pained, as if his attempt at recall hurts him in a physical way. Perhaps it does. Perhaps that is what it feels like. Straining for something that is no longer there.

The man throws his cigarette on the ground, stands on it. 'Well, I hope you don't have far to go.'

Mr B shakes his head. 'No, not far.'

'Local, are you?'

'Harold's Cross.' This reply alarms me. Mr B grew up in Harold's Cross. He hasn't lived there in fifty years.

'You're not walking to Harold's Cross,' says the man. More of a statement than a question. 'Sure that's the other side of the city.'

Mr B's phone rings again and this time, he searches for it, patting his pockets before finding it in the inside zip pocket of his jacket. The man touches his temple with the tip of his index finger and opens the door of the pub. For a moment we are bathed in light and heat and noise. It lasts just long enough to remind me of how cold I am. How wet and hungry. I am not a big fan of the kibble the vet recommends, but still, that is what I see in my mind's eye now. My bowl overflowing with those hard, brown kernels. Saliva forms on my tongue and runs in lines from my mouth.

Good gracious, I appear to be drooling. Yes I am. I'm drooling!

By the time Mr B presses the green button on his phone. It has stopped ringing. He returns the device to his jacket pocket. I'd say it was Mrs Bolton again. She'll be beside herself with worry by now.

When Mr B pushes his cigarette butt into the metal ashtray screwed into the wall beside the door and begins to walk away, I walk after him.

What else can I do?

Chapter Five

We pass the builders' supplies place in Santry where Mr B used to go to buy the materials he needed when he did the nixers. Where did the word 'nixer' come from? If I were Clara or Peter, I'd Google it, I suppose. Sometimes I wonder what it must be like to live in a world where there is an answer for everything. Push a few buttons and there you have it.

The world has changed since I was a pup and not for the better, it seems to me. I know what you're thinking. I'm just an old dog who hasn't learned any new tricks in quite some time.

Mr B did nixers after he got the lump. Mrs Bolton was not pleased to say the least. It wasn't about the nixers or the fact of his retirement. What bothered her was that Mr B didn't ask her opinion. 'People . . . couples . . . *discuss* these things. Normal couples have conversations. They weigh up the pros and cons. That is what people do. *Normal* people.'

He put his hands on either side of her face and kissed her mouth. That took the wind out of her sails.

A group of Mr B's workmates took early retirement at the same time. The company gathered the men in a room to hand out watches and make speeches. The men were told to keep in touch with each other. Not to go to the pub every day and if they did, not to go until after dinner. Mr B didn't keep in touch with anyone. Perhaps he didn't need to. He was busy with his nixers. He umpired cricket matches. He played a few rounds of golf in the summer and snooker in the winter. He honoured the bar at the cricket club and, when he was in need of a change of scene, at the GAA club. Mrs Bolton booked various getaways. The Costa del Sol, a coach tour in California, the lakes of northern Italy, half-board in Majorca. She booked Supervalu breaks, two night's bed and breakfast and a dinner for €199, midweek. She ironed Mr B's clothes and put them in a suitcase and he showed up at the appointed time on the appointed day and away they went. I'd be packed off to the kennels if Clara couldn't take me. Peter said his house wasn't big enough to swing a cat, let alone a dog. That got him off the hook. Just as well, really. Some people aren't dog people.

Mr B stops at a bus stop shelter. I sit on the ground, even though the pavement is wet and cold and hard. A relief, all the same, taking the weight off my legs. The hip joints act up on damp days and this day is damper than most.

'They won't let you take the little fella onto the bus,' says an elderly lady with short thick hairs sprouting from red mounds on her face. She bends her knees and extends her arm towards me and I think her intention is to pet me. She doesn't quite manage to close the gap between her hand and my head. She nods at me instead and I put my head on my paws and close my eyes for a bit. I could fall asleep right here. Here on the cold, hard ground. I really could.

'No,' says Mr B. 'We're just taking our ease.'

'You look frozen solid,' says the old woman, peering up at Mr B through thick glasses on narrow frames.

'That is a skinny breeze alright,' says Mr B, cupping a hand around his mouth and blowing into it.

'They say it will be icy tonight,' she says, the lines on her face deepening at the idea. 'And the fuel allowance cut to shreds. Gangsters, those TDs. They'd let us freeze to death, so they would. Suit them down to the ground, to get us off the books.'

'Gangsters, alright,' says Mr B.

'Are you going to answer that?' She nods towards the sound of his phone, ringing again.

'I think it is broken,' he says.

A bus roars towards us and screeches to a stop, emitting a huge cloud of black, foul-smelling smoke. The old lady grips the handrail inside the door of the bus and pulls herself towards the driver, who doesn't look when she raises her travel pass for inspection.

The driver looks at Mr B. 'Are you coming or going?' he says, his jaws working a wad of chewing gum around his mouth.

'Oh, no . . . I'm . . . just . . .'

The bus door snaps shut and rattles away and I can't help thinking about the little old lady, struggling towards a seat like a ball in a pinball machine. Still, at least when I'm worrying about her I'm not dwelling on our situation which, it seems to me, is not getting any better.

Mr B looks at his watch and frowns, taps the face with his finger, looks at it again, shakes his head. He often does this, as if the hands of the watch have stopped moving, or perhaps the battery has died. But the watch is fine. I have a feeling that it is Mr B's notion of time that is in a state of disrepair. He seems surprised at its passing, as if he hasn't noticed it slipping by. And perhaps that is the case. Perhaps that is part of the disease. Another little gift.

We step away from the shelter of the bus stop and walk on. The traffic is easing now. My best guess of where we are – Whitehall, perhaps -- and how long it has taken us to get here (three hours, I'd say, judging by the ache in my back legs) and the fact that we usually leave for our afternoon promenade around 4 pm, means it must be around 7 pm. No wonder my tummy is grumbling.

We walk for a long time. The ringing and beeping of the phone becomes a soundtrack to this promenade. A background noise. After a while, even I don't notice it anymore. Mr B's breath is laboured. He begins to cough regularly. A sore, chesty sound. Sometimes he has to stop and bend with the force of the cough. Grip something, like a lamppost or railings.

Passersby glance at him as they walk past, coughing and bending, but they don't stop. The ache in the joint of my hind legs has become a piercing pain. I am not a whiner by nature, but I fear the pain will worsen if there is no respite soon.

As a distraction, I force myself to think of something positive. The rain has stopped. I'm certain of its return but, for the moment, its absence is a positive.

When we reach Gardiner Street, Mr B stops and sits on a step outside a guesthouse, even though this makeshift seat offers scant comfort to neither man nor beast. I sit beside him. It is not the kind of street Mr B has any business being on after dark. A tall, gaunt man limps towards us. His hood is pulled over his shaved head and he has the kind of eyes that look vast in the thin, drained landscape of his face. I find myself holding my breath but then the man continues past without so much as a glance in our direction.

Clara is right. One should never judge a book by its cover. Peter would have dismissed the man as a junkie and perhaps a little of his snobbery has brushed off on me over the years. The door of the guesthouse opens and a man appears in its frame. He is short and balding, with pockets of flesh struggling between the buttons of his shirt. 'You can't sit there,' he shouts at us. Mr B remains where he is, staring ahead. The man moves into the light and this serves only to make his appearance worse. The remaining wisps of hair on his head are thin and colourless and his face appears to have burst its banks. The cheeks, jaw and neck merge into one flaccid feature. The effect makes his eyes tiny. I am unable to comment on their colour. I ty

imagine he works in this establishment, judging by his dark trousers and white shirt and black waistcoat. He has the thick, potholed nose of a man who is no stranger to after-hours staff drinks. If Mr B has heard the man, he gives no indication. 'Get up out of there, before I call the police,' the man says, his voice louder now as he comes down the steps. Mr B turns his face towards the man, who says 'Oh' in a quieter voice.

'That used to be a snooker hall,' says Mr B. 'Just over there.' He indicates the place with a nod of his head and the man follows Mr B's gaze to a building with a coffee shop on the ground floor. There are what look like offices on the first and second floors, with strips of bright lights and sets of cream vertical blinds across the windows. 'That is where myself and Christopher played, you know. Taught him everything I know in there. He turned into a handy

40

player in the end. Could beat me on a good day, the jammy little chancer.'

'Carroll's, was it?' Away from the glare of light at the door, the man seems less crabby than before, the brick red of his face eased by shadows. He pushes his hands into the pockets of his trousers as he studies the building across the road. 'That was a hell of a long time ago.'

Mr B nods, puts his hand on my head and scratches behind my ears in an absentminded way. He shakes his head. 'Carroll's was the name of the fella who ran it. The name over the door was "The Green Baize", remember?'

This is not one of Mr B's remaining stories. It is not a story, as such. Just a fact. A snippet of information that has somehow survived in memory after the wrecking ball has demolished most of everything else. Here's what I never understand about this disease. Why that piece of information? Why does he remember that and not, for example, what year it is? Or the day of the week? *The Green Baize*. This has found a foothold on the wall of memory when everything else has fallen away. Perhaps it has to do with Christopher. His brother. Gone to his reward, God rest him. Perhaps it is because Christopher died before Mr B's memory gave way. He remembers that Christopher was clever. That he was an accountant. 'Good with numbers,' he says. I remember Christopher as a reserved man, hidden behind the spread of a newspaper. Still, I only knew him in the last few years of his life. Mr B remembers him as a brother and perhaps there is a bond between brothers that one cannot forget.

Or maybe it is more to do with snooker. After all, Mr B invested years of his life playing the game. Or at least that is what Mrs Bolton would have you believe.

'You look cold,' says the man then, surprising me with the gentleness of the observation. 'You can come in. Have a bowl of soup, if you like. I'd say Chef might be able to find a bone for your companion there, if I ask her nicely.'

Mr B shakes his head, struggles to his feet. 'We'd best be going,' he says. 'Don't want to be late.' This is news to me. We're going somewhere. We don't want to be late. This is good news. Although a bone would have been most welcome.

But good news all the same.

Chapter Six

Mr B displays clips of his life in the garage. Newspaper cuttings, yellow now, tacked to the walls, about a cricket match alongside a picture of him and the Leinster team. There are three neat rows of bright young men in cricket whites. A photograph of Mr B giving the annual speech as president of the Malahide Cricket Club. He is dressed in a navy blazer with the club crest stitched over the breast pocket. A picture of Mrs Bolton smiling towards the camera. She is barefoot on a beach, wearing tight tartan jeans. Her hair falls across one eye with the carelessness of youth. I know it is her because he has written her name on a piece of masking tape underneath the photograph. *Becca*.

An entire shelf is cluttered with tarnished trophies. First place, many of them. Little gold figures bent across snooker tables. Or peering down the shaft of a seven iron. Or crouched behind a wicket. 'If I played Tiddlywinks, I'd want to win.' That is what he used to say, Mr B. 'No point playing unless you're playing to win.'

A card from Rachel, Clara's youngest. *Happy Birthday Papa. Love from Rachel*, scrawled in pencil underneath a sketch of a man (Mr B, I imagine) and a little girl (Rachel, I'd guess) holding hands and smiling wide, single-line smiles. The sun is a huge circle overhead and, beside it, a dog of uncertain breed, seemingly unaware of the laws of gravity. Still, I suppose it is nice to be included.

In the daytime, the Spire in O'Connell Street seems like a monumental waste of time. But at night, something changes. Perhaps because of the street lights. How they reflect and move against the steel. I look up. Its height is impressive. One can only imagine its tip, plunging through the cloud and the smog, straining towards the impossible stars and the inky sky. Heaven, even. They say there is no heaven for dogs but how do they know? How does anybody know anything about afterwards? I don't think Mr B believes. He used to say, after a few beverages, when he was inclined to get maudlin, 'Lower me down the mossy bank and that is a wrap.'

Now, he says three Hail Marys before he goes to bed every night. An insurance policy perhaps. Just in case.

They go to mass every Sunday, himself and Mrs Bolton. But I suspect that has something to do with what Mrs B calls 'putting in the day'. The time between morning and night can stretch like elastic when memory has let you down.

Now, I've lost all track of time. It is night. Has been for ages. That is all I know. And we're walking. We're still walking. The mobile device in Mr B's jacket has stopped ringing and beeping. 'Out of juice,' as Mr B would say. The phone is old and the battery life isn't what it once was.

In my outer vision, I see the rhythm of Mr Bolton's shoes. The ones Mrs Bolton bought for him last Christmas. Slip-ons so there is no need for getting into knots with laces and zips. The pinstriped socks Clara gave him for his birthday. She finally stopped buying him books. Perhaps she saw the dusty pile on his bedside locker one day. Biographies and historical non-fiction. His areas of interest. World War II. The Black and Tans. Mussolini. The Blueshirts. Imperial Russia in all its pomp and glory. I imagine all those pages he read. All those words. I wonder where they are. If they're anywhere. Sealed somewhere in a pocket of brain tissue. Buried like treasure that will never again be found.

The shoes gleam in the streetlight as if they've been freshly polished, which is not unlikely. This is one chore that Mr B remembers and perhaps even relishes although that could be related to his memory of it. The fact that it is intact, this memory. The location of the polish and brushes. Which colour he needs for which pair of shoes. The choosing of the brushes, one to clean and one to shine. He hasn't forgotten any of it. Perhaps this task has become a celebration of what remains.

The gates into St Stephen's Green are closed. Locked. He peers into the park, through the iron bars of the gates. He seems tired, leaning against the bars. Disappointed too. As if the closed gates are a bother to the carefully timed agenda in Mr B's head. He bends his knees and lowers himself until he is seated on the ground. I sit beside him. When I open my mouth, my tongue unfurls and hangs, limp and dry.

If someone tosses a coin towards us, I will not be surprised.

A police car trawls by, the officer in the passenger seat twisting his head this way and that as if he is trying to find something. Or someone. Perhaps us. Myself and Mr B. It is possible that Mrs Bolton will have notified the guards by now. Mr B never goes anywhere without her now. Other than his walks with me. But these are mainly round the block affairs, the shop being the farthest we've been in years.

I bark to attract the police officer's attention. He doesn't hear me. My bark doesn't have the impact it once did, I'm afraid. A yap now, you might say. Mr B puts his hand on my head, pulls at my ears in what he thinks is a soothing manner. But there is no soothing me now. We are in crisis. It may sound melodramatic but, given the normally slow nature of our lives, I believe it is not an overstatement. Crisis. A state of chassis, Sean O'Casey called it.

We are missing.

One might say that Mr B has been missing for years.

Chapter Seven

It began with directions. The way to Dundalk. They'd been going there for years, to visit Mrs B's elderly aunt who lived alone. 'Splendid isolation,' she called it. She had become infirm following a hip operation. As I arranged myself in my usual spot by the window in the back seat, Mrs Bolton spoke to Mr B about a particular nursing home she favoured. The cost of it and the long-term outlook for her aunt's hip. Mr B drove to the end of the Millview Road and stopped. Looked left and right. I did too, as is my habit. No traffic either way. Still, he idled there and drummed his fingers against the wheel.

'And I told the consultant that Aunt Joan couldn't possibly . . .' Mrs Bolton stopped talking. Stopped right there. She never did finish that sentence. I never found out what Aunt Joan couldn't possibly do.

'What are you doing?' she asked him.

'Ummm?' he answered, in a way that suggested he was buying himself some time.

'Why aren't you going?' She said, looking left and right, checking that there were no cars coming.

'We're going to Dundalk you said.' Not quite a question.

'Yes, of course we're going to Dundalk.' Wariness had crept into her tone.

'Good, yes, that is what I thought.' He nodded. Still the car didn't move.

'For God's sake, Ted. There is a line of cars behind us now. Will you move!'

'We are turning right . . . aren't we?' He indicated right. Waited.

When she looked at him, there was worry on her face. A hint of fear. Then a car behind us beeped and she nodded and he turned right and the car moved off.

The rest of the journey passed without incident. He knew every turn. Even the name of the roads. But that right turn. That was the first one. For Mrs Bolton, it was probably the worst one. For him too, I daresay. Because he knew back then. What was what.

He still knew.

Chapter Eight

I'm thinking about the medication now. The tablets. Six in the morning, one at night. Lipostat. That is the name of the one he swallows in the evening. 'Have I taken my Lipostat?' He asks that question every night. After the nine o'clock news. 'Have I taken my Lipostat?' It is a tricky word to remember. Lipostat. But he retains it somehow.

He hasn't taken his Lipostat tonight and, at the rate we're going, he won't be home to take the six tomorrow morning. It is late now. There is a sign for

Sandymount. We are the only ones on the footpath. An occasional car on the road. Mr B is limping now, as well as coughing. We keep walking, although our headway is slower than before.

The rain returns, softer than before. A drizzle.

Mrs Bolton sometimes wonders what might happen if he stopped taking the tablets. I've overheard her saying it to Clara, over a cup of tea. And no, I'm not an eavesdropper. One can't help hearing things when one sits under a kitchen table hoping for a windfall of Hobnobs. I'm very fond of Hobnobs, even though they can disagree with my constitution.

Mrs Bolton is mistrustful of medication. She is reluctant to take even a Panadol when she has a headache. Side effects. That is what she worries about. She reads the information leaflets that come inside the boxes of his pills. *Nightmares, depression, headaches, dizziness, insomnia, blurred vision* . . . Still, she pours them into a plastic tumbler every morning, hands him a glass of water, watches as he shakes them into his mouth. She checks for the telltale rise and fall of his Adam's apple beneath the skin of his neck. He was not always so obedient. Now he does everything she says. She has become his compass. His way of navigating the world.

We're on the beach now, my paws sinking into the soft, wet sand at the water's edge. Mr B stops to light a cigarette. When I look behind I see the line of his footsteps and beside them, the heart-shaped pattern of my prints. There is no sound, other than the labour of our breathing and the suck and hiss of small waves, lapping the shore like a mother's tongue.

Ahead, there is a lifeguard's hut. These are usually taken away after the summer season but this one looks like it has been forgotten. The roof is sagging and rust is running riot. Mr B strikes out towards it and I follow.

Sandymount does not feature in any of the remaining stories. However, he used to mention it as the place he learned to swim. His mother took him and his six siblings across town on the bus from Harold's Cross. She'd pack a picnic. Corned beef sandwiches and fruit cake and a flask of tea. Is that why we're here now?

Seven children, Mr B's mother had. Not counting the miscarriages. You didn't count those, back then. I believe it was considered the norm in those days and never mentioned. Mrs Bolton is not fond of the story that Mr B still tells. It concerns his mother, who walked to the church one day to seek advice from the parish priest. He was an enormous slab of a man with a shock of white hair. He left a constant whiff of alter wine in his wake. Mr B's mother wanted advice about family planning. She knelt in the narrow darkness of the confessional and waited for the grid to slide back. She waited for the outline of his face to form as her eyes adjusted to the gloom. Her reasons were economic, in the main. But also, I imagine, she felt the strain of so many dependants. Look at my own poor mother. Worn away after giving birth to the six of us. We were her third, and last, litter. I am grateful for my gender. I will never know that pain. That sacrifice.

The priest told Mr B's mother to go home and not to darken his door again with such notions. He said it was a sin. Denying a man his married rights.

The lifeguard's hut would be better described as a shack, listing and creaking like a death rattle. Still, it is true to say that it affords some shelter from the sharp needles of rain. The high-pitched wind rushes at us, wrenching the breath from our mouths.

Inside, the air is layered with the smell of stale urine in spite of the ventilation. Mr B sits on the floor and I sit beside him, ignoring the dirt and the debris. Or perhaps I'm beyond caring about such things. The relief of taking the weight off my paws is vast. Mr B feels it too. I can tell by the sound he makes when he sits beside me, leaning his back against the wall of the hut. A rasping sound, laden with gratitude. His head nods towards his chest.

Outside, the cry of a seagull is flung about by the wind. A mournful sound. I press my body against the length of Mr B's leg to coax some warmth to flow between us. Sleep is like an elusive lover that one yearns for. I lift my head and look through the space where the door used to be.

From here, home seems a long way away.

Chapter Nine

In the morning, we set off again. My hopes of going home dim as Mr B follows the canal over the Leeson Street Bridge, onto Charlemont and past Portobello. I remember the names of the bridges from when Clara had to learn them for a geography test she did in primary school. Some people think my breed is a vain one with not much in the way of intellect, but my memory is as good as any Border Collie, no matter what those smug canines would have you believe. We turn left at the

Robert Emmet Bridge and keep going until we reach Harold's Cross. He walks with the dazed confusion of a sleepwalker. Fellow walkers have to give way to us. He stops often, to bend and cough, pat my head.

The house where Mr B grew up has gone.

The park is still here, I recognise it from Mr B's descriptions long ago. The compact nature of it. The strange shape of it and the way it appears to have been dropped in the middle of the road by someone who didn't give it much thought. He finds a bench. I sit on the ground beside him. A cat watches me from a flowerbed. On the air, the aroma of sausages, sizzling on a pan. I lie down.

The chemist shop next door to the house is gone too. The pharmacist and his wife lived over the shop. They had no children. There was a large, beautifully manicured back garden where they grew apples and pears. A vast array of berries too. The popular ones, of course. Strawberries and raspberries. And the ones you don't hear much about anymore. Loganberries and gooseberries.

And here we come to one of Mr B's remaining stories. The story features the chemist's wife, Mrs Scott. She was a heavyset woman in A-line tweed skirts. She had long, thin hair that she put up in a bun with elastic. She picked the fruit from the trees and bushes in her garden and arranged them in a wicker basket. Then, she hefted the basket on top of the wall that divided her garden from the Bolton family's garden. Later, Mr B's mother lifted the basket down. She offered the ripe fruit to her children and made a crumble with the leftovers. She pocketed the two shiny sixpences at the bottom of the basket without commenting on their presence. Mr B, her eldest son, witnessed this silent transaction between the two women. Somehow he understood that his mother accepted these small coins because there was no choice. That if she had the freedom of choice, the basket might have remained on the wall, untouched, the fruit sweetly rotting inside.

In spite of the fruit gifted to them, Mr B remembers climbing the wall, plucking more fruit from the branches while Mr and Mrs Scott pedalled their wares in the chemist's shop. I suppose it is a boy's rite of passage. The nectar of the forbidden fruit is perhaps sweeter than that which is given.

The house is now a used car lot. So too is the chemist shop. The gardens and the fruit trees survive only in Mr B's memory. One of the last remaining stories. Perhaps it is the one that will endure when the others have fallen away, given the vividness with which Mr B remembers the details.

The day is already drawing to a conclusion as we reach Mount Jerome Cemetery. Mr B reaches for one of the bars of the entrance gate. He holds on tight as if he might fall. Perhaps he might. He hasn't eaten anything since lunchtime yesterday and heaven knows, his body holds no reserves for such prolonged deprivation.

On one side of the gate, a man sells hot drinks from a little van. The smell of coffee beans wafts towards us, earthy and strong and, perhaps for the first time, I understand why people drink it. On the crisp air, the aroma sounds a wholesome note, like a promise of something.

I'm being fanciful. I've drunk only rainwater since we left and the idea of a bowl of kibble and the creak of my wicker basket by the cooker fills me with longing. I shoo it from my mind. 'Live in the moment,' Clara advises.

She's a counsellor now. How proud I was the day of her graduation. Not that I was there, of course not. But I often look at the photograph of her in the black cap and gown. It is fading in its frame on the wall in the front room from the rays of the morning sun. 'Pretty as a picture,' Mr B says when the photograph catches his attention. It could be construed as vanity, given the fact that Clara is the image of her father as a young man, although perhaps he has forgotten how he used to be.

The man selling the coffee and tea sweeps his eyes along the entrance to the graveyard. His gaze moves across us and then back, settling on myself and Mr B. Taking us in.

'You look like you could do with a hot drop,' he says after a while.

'A hot drop of what?' Mr B asks.

'I've only coffee or tea. Nothing stronger than that, I'm afraid.' The man shakes his head and smiles and Mr B mimics him, shaking his head and smiling too.

'Cup of rosy do you?'

'Rosy Lee?' Mr B smiles properly now, recognising the reference. Rosy Lee. Tea.

The man nods, reaches for a paper cup, throws a teabag into the bottom of it, with his bare fingers, I might add, no gloves. He presses a green button that spits hot water. Mr B pats the pockets of his coat and trousers. 'I'm not sure if I brought my . . .'

'On the house,' the man says. 'Given the day that is in it.'

'Is it Christmas day?' Mr B looks worried now, perhaps realising for the first time that we are not where we are supposed to be. That we are far from home.

'No, no, no, don't be worrying. Plenty of time to get the turkey and ham in. No, it is . . . it is me ma's anniversary.' He nods towards the graveyard. 'Five years ago today, she met her maker.'

'Down the mossy bank,' says Mr B.

'What?' A frown twists at one side of the tea man's face.

'Thirty-three years. That is how long I worked at the airport, you know.'

The man's attention is turned by a woman arriving at the van. She is in her sixties perhaps. She looks sedate in a long wool coat. A silk scarf is knotted around her slender neck. She wears tiny black patent shoes with a hint of a heel. She wants coffee. 'An Americano,' she says. While the man busies himself, she bends her head to the posy of white carnations lying along the bend of her arm. When she smells the flowers, she nods, satisfied, and waits for her drink.

I wonder what we are going to do next.

Mr B pours three sachets of sugar into his tea. Mrs Bolton would take a dim view of that, if she could see him. Doctor Martin says he's to cut down but I wonder, where is the harm now? Although it certainly is not for the likes of me to presume to know more than a medical professional.

Still, the sugar might give him a boost. And the drink will warm him. He looks bloodless, as if all there is beneath his skin is a shaky series of bones, one gripping another, wobbly as a house of cards.

He takes two sips and puts the cup on the ground. He struggles to his feet.

'It is nearly closing time,' the tea man calls after him. Mr B doesn't stop. He moves soundlessly into the graveyard and the tea man looks pointedly at the abandoned cup and throws his eyes skyward. He accompanies the movement with a jaded exhalation of breath. It is odd to think that he will be the one to find us.

To think of the compassion he will demonstrate, come the morning.

Chapter Ten

The cemetery is vast. We never reach its boundary, despite the range of our meanderings between the graves and vaults. He never finds his mother's grave. Nor Christopher's. I assume that is what he is looking for although I could be wrong. I've been wrong about many things. Miss Cavendish, for instance. She was my first mistake. One is more trusting when one is young.

I thought that once he saw the house and garden were gone, we would go home.

Instead, here we are, dragging our weary bones through this maze of the departed. A bell rings, its tone cutting into the sharp cold of night. Perhaps it signals the closure of the cemetery. Mr B pays no attention. He continues to walk despite the strain of each step, a grimace etched across his face. Finally he stops, rests his back against a headstone and slides downwards until he reaches the ground. His eyes close. I move towards him and paw at his coat. I whine in a way that is certainly not in keeping with my character. It is not superstition. Or a fear of ghosts or spirits. I don't go in for any of that claptrap. But a graveyard is no place for the living once the gates have been closed and the dark has settled for the night.

I whine and I paw. After a while, I sit beside Mr B and, when I realise that he's asleep, I pick my way onto his lap, arrange myself in a tight circle. I am not normally tactile but this situation is no longer normal. It stopped being normal when we walked out of Mrs O'Connell's shop and turned right instead of left.

I think I sleep. When I awake, my tongue is dangling from my mouth and it takes effort to reel it in. Mr B's head is on the ground now, one of his hands trapped beneath it. The fingers of his other hand is tucked inside my collar, cold as stone.

I untangle myself from his fingers. I push my nose around his head and lick his face. I am not in the habit of licking people. I know lots of my kind do it, but I never saw the point, truth be told. Some might say I have kept my emotions in check, but I believe that Mr B is aware of the high esteem in which I hold him. No, this licking is not a signal of my affection but rather one of practicality. Perhaps I might revive him in this way. I am not keen on his pallor. Nor of his breath which is as threadbare as a tramp's overcoat.

I lick his face again, my tongue bumping along the rough terrain of his chin where the stubble has taken hold. He moans, which gives me hope as the sound has substance to it. 'Life in the old dog yet,' Mr B used to say when he could still give Peter a run for his money at snooker.

He never let the children win. I've heard him confess it, with no regret in his tone. 'They had to learn,' he said.

When his memory of the game began to dim and his technique suffered, Peter was his father's son, winning every break while Mr B watched and wondered what was happening to him.

They never told him, you know. That he had Alzheimer's. No, that is not true. Clara mentioned it once. She took him to Kealy's for breakfast. That was back when he still had an appetite. She waited until he was wiping the last of the egg yolk off his plate with a piece of bread. Then she dropped the bombshell. 'What did he say?' Mrs Bolton – who had been against the idea – asked when they got home. Clara shrugged. 'He just . . . sort of nodded and drank his tea and told me about the day he got the "lump".' Mrs Bolton nodded. 'It is probably because you brought him to Kealy's,' she said. 'It might have been a distraction since that was where . . .'

'That was where he went the minute he got the "lump".' Clara finished the sentence.

'Cheque in my arse pocket, jacket on and I was out of there. Middle of the morning. Didn't tell any of them. Didn't say a word.' Mrs Bolton nearly sings it.

'Didn't give a tuppenny damn. Sat on the stool. Pint when you're ready. Ten o'clock in the morning,' says Clara.

They smile at each other, perhaps because of the familiarity of the words and their chanting of them. They recited the lines like nursery rhymes.

Apart from that, they never mentioned it. That word. Alzheimer's. He is lucky, Mr B. Having Mrs Bolton to look after him. And Peter the odd time. And Clara of course, when Mrs Bolton manages to get away on a bridge weekend, or perhaps a city break with her sister.

Mrs Bolton fell in love with him when he was dashing and handsome and charming and unreliable. Now, he is old and frail and afraid. And still she loves him. *For better or worse.* That is what she said. What she promised.

I try to stand, stretch my legs a bit but I can't manage. A combination of stiff joints that comes with old age, and tiredness and cold. It is the coldest part of the night, just before dawn. I can see a faint outline of the horizon that signals the return of the sun. I feel a surge of hope when I see that thin blue line out there, at the edge of the world. It is what I imagine the human spirit might feel like. A surge of hope. Even when truth is bearing down on you.

This is the last story. I'm quite certain. I settle myself in the bend of Mr B's elbow, put my face close to his. He is still, and white, and cold. His mouth is curved in a small, stiff smile. One might think he was merely asleep. Dreaming perhaps. That he has found the place where his memories live. He is lifting them, one by one, blowing the dust from them, opening them with careful fingers. He knows their worth now. He looks inside.

Remembers everything. All over again.